For my parents, who have encouraged all my adventures,
and for Brian, the best adventure partner. -S.G.

For Sara, who encouraged me to make stories
and drawings from doodles. -B.S.

Edited by Lily Coyle
Illustrated by Brian Schmidt
Production editor: Hanna Kjeldbjerg

ISBN 13: 978-1-64343-885-6
Library of Congress Catalog Number: 9781643438856
Printed in the United States of America
First Printing: 2020
24 23 22 21 20   5 4 3 2 1

Beaver's Pond Press
7108 Ohms Lane
Edina, MN 55439–2129
(952) 829-8818
www.BeaversPondPress.com
To order, call (800)-901-3480. Reseller discounts available.

To order, visit www.lowerwoodlandstudio.com. Reseller discounts available.

Contact Brian Schmidt and Sara Galm at www.lowerwoodlandstudio.com for art prints, school visits, speaking engagements,
freelance writing projects, and interviews.

ABC Adventures
with
Fuzzlewump and Grizzlegrump

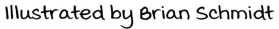

Illustrated by Brian Schmidt

Written by Sara Galm

A is for apple picking right when you wake.

B is for **boating** across a cool lake.

C is for **collecting** bugs, shells, and more.

D is for **digging** to a faraway shore.

E is for entering, no matter the fright . . .

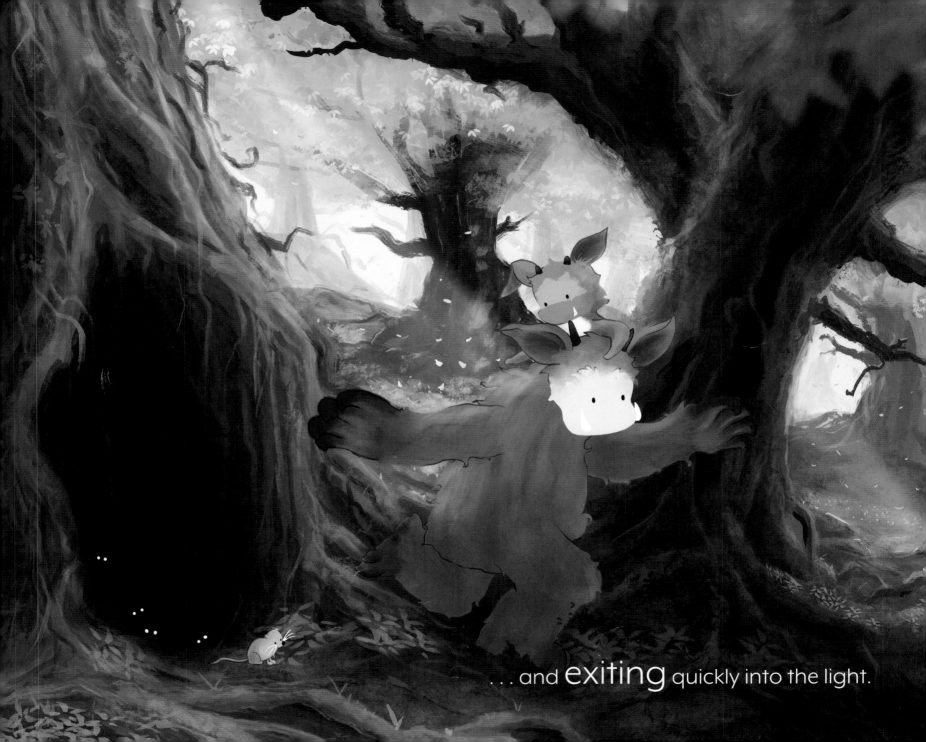

. . . and **exiting** quickly into the light.

F is for **fishing** for big fish and small.

G is for gardening—
a bounty for all.

H is for **hunting** with swords and with shields.

I is for **imagining** while lying in fields.

J is for jumping over lava so hot.

K is for karate on this mountaintop spot

L is for love aglow in the skies.

M is for **mummy,** dressing up in disguise.

N is for navigating dangerous lands.

O is for **orbiting**
space, holding hands.

P is for **parachuting** out of the sky.

Q is for **quietly** tiptoeing by.

R is for **racing** so steady and swift.

S is for **skiing** straight through a snowdrift.

T is for telephone at the top of a tree.

U is for upside down, feeling so free.

V is for vines swinging in the breeze.

W is for white-water rafting with ease.

X is for **X** marks the spot with the treasure.

Y is for **yodeling** loudly with pleasure.

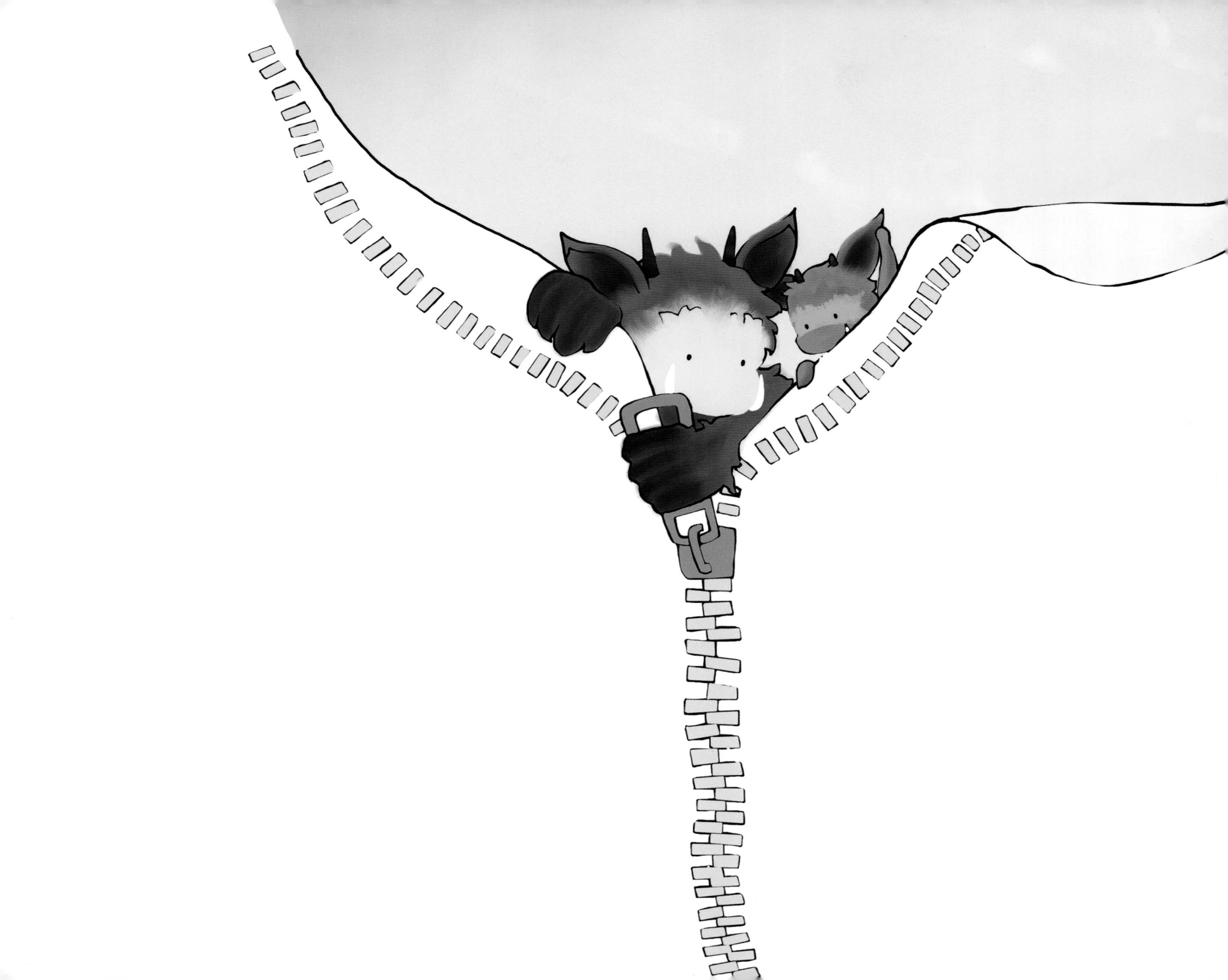

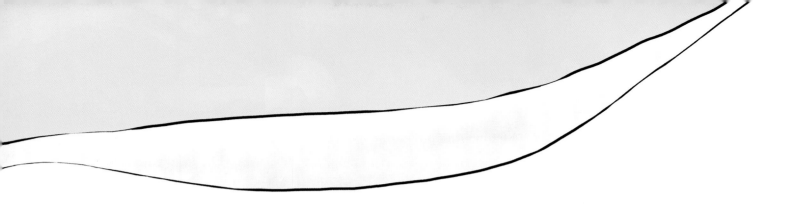

Z is for **zipping** the zipper up high.

Now is the time we must say good-bye!

About the Author + Illustrator:

Sara and Brian's adventure began when they met in New York City in 2011. Since then, they've gone on all of life's adventures together in search of the things they value most: nature, kindness, humor, and love. Today, they live and create together in the Twin Cities in Minnesota.

To see more of their art and books, visit www.lowerwoodlandstudio.com with a parent or guardian.

Design Your Own Adventure . . .

1. Decide who will be your adventure buddy.

2. Pick your adventure destination.

3. Imagine what you might discover!

Adventure Possibilities

- ☐ Visit a beach and collect shells.
- ☐ Pick fruit at an orchard.
- ☐ Go stargazing and make s'mores.
- ☐ Hike a hill and sing your favorite song.
- ☐ Build a fort out of sticks or snow.
- ☐ Plant a garden and help it grow.
- ☐ _____
- ☐ _____
- ☐ _____

The Travels of
Fuzzlewump and Grizzlegrump